How Big Is Love?

Emma Dodd

templar books

an imprint of Candlewick Press

Before you came, I did not know
just how big love could be.

It's wider than the ocean;
it's deeper than the sea.

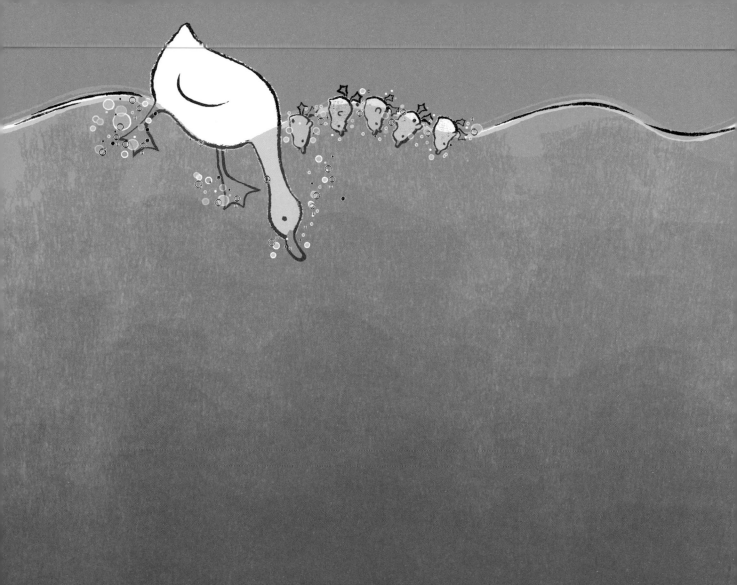

Love's taller than the mountains.
It stretches way up high.

Farther than the farthest star,

way beyond the sky.

Love goes on and on and on.
It fills your heart and mine.

Love's brighter than
the brightest light.

It makes the
whole world shine.

Love never, ever changes,
no matter what life brings.

Love lifts you up when you are down.
It helps you find your wings.

Love is all around you
every single day.

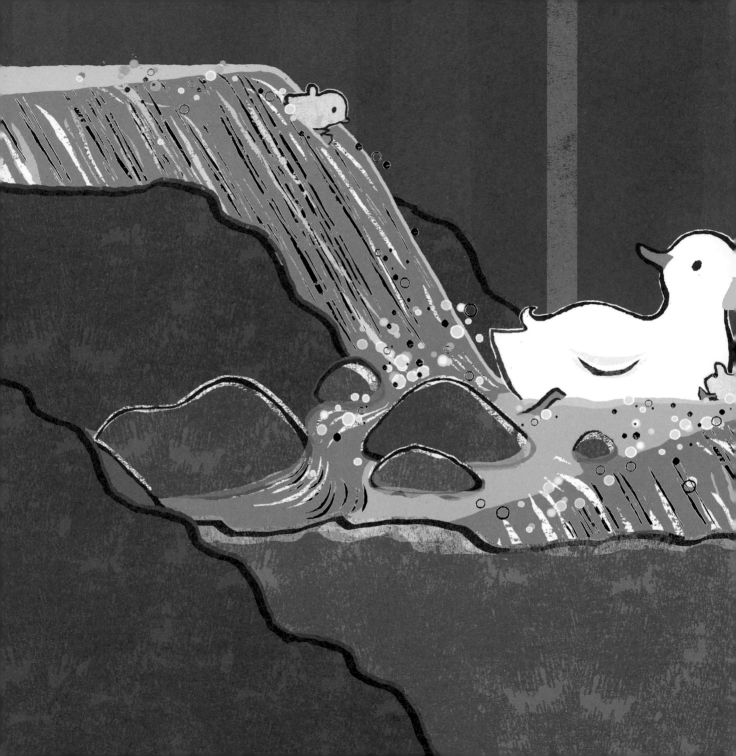

And even when life gets hard,
love never goes away.

And you, my loves, have taught me
what I know to be true:
there is nothing bigger than
the love I feel for you.

For Maddy Bard, who knows how big love is.

First US edition 2020
First UK edition published by Templar Books,
an imprint of Bonnier Books (UK) 2021
Library of Congress Catalog Card Number pending
ISBN 978-1-5362-1544-1

20 21 22 23 24 25 LEO 10 9 8 7 6 5 4 3 2 1

Printed in Heshan, Guangdong, China

This book was typeset in Eureka Sans.
The illustrations were created digitally.

TEMPLAR BOOKS
an imprint of
Candlewick Press
99 Dover Street
Somerville, Massachusetts 02144

www.candlewick.com